Spring Break Safari

by Christine Peymani

Bath · New York · Singapore · Hong Kong · Cologne · Delhi · Melbourne

First published by Parragon in 2007
Parragon
Queen Street House
4 Queen Street
Bath BA1 1HE, UK

ISBN 978-1-4054-8728-3

Printed in China

Chapter 1

"And those are just some of the wonders of the majestic rainforest!" announced Miss Couri, the Stiles High Biology teacher. She had just finished showing her class a slideshow from her recent trip to the tropical rainforest and, unlike most slideshows, this one had actually been extremely cool, full of exotic animals, unusual plants and stunning landscapes.

"Wow, I never knew trees could be so awesome," Cloe whispered to her best friend, Yasmin.

"Oh, I did!" Yasmin replied. "I've always loved trees."

"Those plants and animals were beautiful," agreed their best friend Jade, who was sitting right behind Cloe. "In fact, seeing all those spectacular colours gave me some great new fashion ideas!"

"I'm glad you girls are excited," their teacher said, overhearing them. "Because I'm planning an eco-tour to the rainforest over spring break, and I'll be taking a group of eight students with me."

"I'm there!" cried Sasha from her seat behind Yasmin, then clapped her hand over her mouth, realizing how loud she'd been. She was the fourth in this quartet of best friends, and tended to be the decision-maker of the group.

"We'll go mountain climbing, take nature hikes and kayak down the river," Miss Couri continued. "We'll also get to study the local wildlife and help with conservation efforts in the rainforest."

"That sounds amazing," gushed Yasmin. "I can't imagine a better way to spend our spring break."

The bell rang, signalling the end of the school day, and Miss Couri called, "I do hope you'll think about the trip. I'll have a sign-up sheet here tomorrow."

Miss Couri was one of the newest, youngest and hippest teachers at Stiles High. As they hurried out of the classroom, the girls excitedly discussed what a fun trip leader she would be.

"She always seems so excited about what she's teaching us!" Cloe exclaimed. "I mean, she manages to make biology fun, so with something as awesome as the rainforest, I'm sure we'll be, blown away!"

"Cloe, biology is fun!" Yasmin protested. She was the best student of the group, and although creative writing was more her

3

thing, she loved all her classes. "And rainforests are all about biology – the plants, the animals, the ecosystems…that was the point of Miss Couri's presentation today, not just to show us pretty pictures!"

"School's over, Yas – no more lectures, okay?" Cloe protested.

"I just think if we're seriously considering this trip, then we should be clear on what we're getting ourselves into," Yasmin explained. "I mean, it sounds like a fabulous adventure, but like Miss Couri said, we'd really be studying the rainforest."

"Wait, you don't think she'd actually give us homework on this trip, do you?" Jade asked as the girls headed for the parking lot. "I mean, it is spring break – that's time off from school, not time for more school!"

"It's an educational trip," Sasha replied, "so yeah, I think there might be some learning involved. But we'd be learning about amazing creatures, like jaguars and monkeys and toucans, and getting to see them first-hand! So it'll be way more fun than an average class."

"Plus we'd get to visit a spectacular place, and we'd have way cooler stories to tell than if we just went to the beach like we usually do for spring break," Yasmin added as they piled into Cloe's cruiser. "And we'd get to help save the rainforest."

"That does sounds awesome," Jade agreed.

"So, where to, ladies?" Cloe asked, sliding behind the wheel.

"It's such a beautiful day – do you want to go to the park?" Yasmin suggested, tilting her head back to soak in the sun.

"Yeah!" her friends agreed.

Cloe drove them to the park, where they gathered around a picnic table facing the

Stilesville Mall, one of their absolute favourite places in town. "It feels weird to be so close to the mall and not go in," Jade joked.

"I know," Cloe replied. "But it really is too pretty out for us to be cooped up inside."

"Guess I'll just have to pray for a cloudy day!" Jade teased.

"Well, if we do sign up for this trip, we'll need a whole new set of safari attire," Sasha pointed out.

©MGA

"That's it, I'm in!" Jade declared. "Anything for a new wardrobe." She swept her hand in front of her as though painting a picture for her friends and continued, "I can see it now – safari chic in cute cargos and camo-prints!"

"Ooh, awesome idea!" Cloe agreed. "Are you girls sure we shouldn't stop into the mall for a quick look around?"

"Cloe! We're enjoying nature, remember?" Sasha chided her.

"Oh…right," Cloe said. "Are you sure we can't enjoy it from inside?" The girls just shook their heads at her and kept talking.

"I really want to go on this trip," Yasmin announced. "Will you girls go with me?"

"Of course!" Sasha replied. "We're a team!"

"But Yasmin, we really need to finish the new issue of Bratz Magazine over spring break," Jade reminded her. "And we haven't even started on it yet!"

A huge smile spread across Yasmin's face. "Jade, that's it!" she declared.

"What's it?" Jade asked, confused.

"We'll do a rainforest-themed issue of Bratz Magazine!" Yasmin squealed. "It'll be so hot, and we'll have tons of amazing activities and fabulous new sights to write about."

"Yeah!" Jade agreed. "And I'll have fabulous new jungle-inspired fashions to share with our readers."

"And we can tell people about all the cool plants and animals that live in the jungle," Yasmin added. "We could really raise awareness about how spectacular the rainforest is."

"I love it!" Cloe exclaimed. "Theme issues are my favourite!"

"So it's settled," Sasha replied. "We'll sign up for the trip first thing in the morning."

"This is going to be the most exciting spring break ever!" Yasmin cried happily.

"And the most spectacular issue of Bratz Magazine, too!" Jade declared.

Chapter 2

"Miss Couri, Miss Couri, we're going on your trip!" Cloe cried, rushing up to her teacher along with her three best friends before their Biology class the next day.

"That's great," their teacher replied. "I know you girls will really enjoy it."

"I know we will!" Yasmin agreed. "I'm always up for helping the environment!"

"The school has agreed to sponsor all eight students on this trip," Miss Couri told them. "In exchange, you'll report back to the rest of the school on what you learned there. Plus you'll be doing a lot of volunteer work to help offset the expense of the expedition. How does that sound?"

"Free sounds great!" Sasha exclaimed.

"And we were planning to do a special issue of our magazine based on our trip, so we'll have plenty of great material to share with all our classmates."

"Perfect!" Miss Couri replied. "Come on into my classroom and I'll hook you up with all the info you need."

She gave the girls permission slips, itineraries and a list of supplies to bring.

"The school will arrange your plane tickets," she explained, "so you don't have to worry about that."

"Are they booking our hotel rooms, too?" Jade asked.

"Actually, we'll be camping out for the whole trip," Miss Couri told her.

Jade looked stunned, "That's cool," she said.

©MGA

I guess I can try roughing it."

"Has anyone else signed up for the trip yet?" Sasha asked.

"Actually, you girls got the last four spots!" Miss Couri handed them her sign-up sheet so they could add their names to the list.

"Oh cool, Fianna's going too!" Cloe exclaimed, noticing their friend's name at the top.

"And do you know Lilee?" Miss Couri inquired. When the girls shook their heads, she told them, "She's a new student here and I don't think she knows anyone else on the trip, so I hope you girls will help her feel welcome."

"Consider us the welcoming committee!" Jade declared. But just then, she noticed the other two names on the list. "Oh no! Kaycee and Kirstee!"

"Where?" Cloe gasped, peering anxiously around the classroom.

"On the sign-up sheet!" Jade explained. "They're going to the rainforest with us!"

"Is there a problem?" Miss Couri wanted to know. "We really need to work together as a team on this trip, so if there are any issues I should know about, you should really tell me now."

"No, no, it's fine," Sasha interrupted. "It's true that Kaycee and Kirstee haven't always been the nicest to us, but we'll manage. After all, we can get along with anyone – right girls?"

Her best friends nodded, but they looked unsure. Kaycee and Kirstee were twins who always seemed to be out to get Sasha, Cloe, Jade and Yasmin. In fact, they were so snotty and mean that they seemed almost like evil twins from a story – which was why the girls called them the 'Tweevils'.

"Well, I'm glad to hear that," Miss Couri replied. "I just know this trip will be a fantastic experience for all of you. I'm so glad to have you on board!"

The bell rang and the girls took their seats. Miss Couri spent the whole class teaching them more about the rainforest, getting the girls even more psyched about their spring break safari.

After school, they found Fianna at her locker and eagerly chatted about the trip with her. "I'm thrilled that you girls are going!" Fianna exclaimed. "I wanted to go anyway, but now I know it will be fun!"

"You're not talking about the rainforest trip, are you?" Kirstee demanded, coming up on them with her identical twin sister at her side. As always, the Tweevils were dressed from head to toe in blinding, fluffy, bubble-gum pink outfits.

"Yeah, 'cause we're going on that trip and we don't want you Bratz ruining it!" Kaycee added.

"Why would you two want to go on that trip?" Jade asked. "You don't even like being outside. And last time I checked, camping and hiking involved a whole lot of time outside."

"Hey, no one said anything about camping!" Kaycee whined. "Kirstee, did you know we'd have to go camping?"

"How would I have known that?" Kirstee snapped. "It's totally gross, but Mum and Dad expect us both to get As in biology, and earning extra credit on this trip is the only chance we've got."

"Miss Couri is giving you extra credit for going on the trip?" Cloe asked. Her Biology grade was okay, but she wouldn't mind a little boost too.

"Sure she will – because we'll be her biggest helpers!" Kirstee declared.

"Yeah, you're always real helpful," Sasha muttered.

"Okay guys, chill," Yasmin whispered to her friends. Then turning to the Tweevils with a dazzling smile she said, "Well, that sounds just great. We'll look forward to working with you!"

"Whatever," the Tweevils replied, and stormed away.

©MGA

"I can't believe we have to spend our spring break with them," the girls heard Kaycee grumble as she headed down the school hallway.

"Yas, what was that burst of Tweevil hospitality all about?" Jade asked once the twins were out of earshot.

"You heard Miss Couri," Yasmin replied. "She expects us all to get along on this trip and I, for one, don't want to miss out on this amazing opportunity just because the Tweevils get on our nerves."

"You're right," Sasha agreed. "And being nice to the Tweevils seems to annoy them even more, so there's definitely an up-side!"

"We'll kill them with kindness," Fianna declared.

"I don't know why we didn't think of it before," Cloe added. "They can't stand nice people!"

"Well, now that we have that resolved, I think it's time to go pick out those cute safari outfits I was talking about," Jade announced.

"Sounds like the perfect way to kick off the weekend!" Sasha agreed.

"Wait, Fianna, do you know the new girl, Lilee?" Yasmin asked.

"No, why?" Fianna asked.

"She's going on the trip too, and I was thinking maybe we should see if she wants to hit the mall with us," Yasmin explained.

"Aw, Yas, that's totally sweet," Fianna told her. "But since none of us have ever met her, our options are either to ask every girl in the school if her name is Lilee, or just to wait till we meet her on the trip."

"I guess you're right," Yasmin said. "It's just that shopping is my favourite way to get to know new friends!"

"Hey, mine too," Cloe agreed. "But I think trekking through the rainforest will be a pretty good bonding experience, too."

"You're probably right," Yasmin admitted, smiling at her friend.

"To the mall!" Jade shouted, and the girls hurried to the parking lot and over to the mall.

They darted into the Stilesville Mall and headed straight for Unique Boutique, one of their favourite shops. In no time, all five girls had picked out graphic tees and cropped cargo pants, military jackets and camo-print caps, plus sporty shoes that were both comfy and chic.

The girls all trooped to the changing room to show off their latest look.

"We are gonna be the hippest explorers the jungle has ever seen!" Jade squealed as her friends emerged from their changing room cubicles. "Cloe, your camo-print top is the cutest!"

"No way, your tiger-logo tee is!" Cloe replied. "Although, Yas, I am totally loving those cargo pants – the lilac accents complement that camouflage pattern so well."

"I know, I'm crazy about these!" Yasmin cried. "But you know what else I'm digging? The metallic stars on Fianna's T-shirt!"

"Thanks!" Fianna said. "But I have to say, Sasha is the one with the truly cutting-edge look – check out that chic khaki skirt!"

Sasha did a quick little twirl in her new skirt. "I know it's not practical enough for the trip, but it looks so good with my new green jacket and camo-print tank that I couldn't resist!"

"That'd look totally hip for school or a

trip to the mall," Jade replied. "Way to bring safari chic to the streets of Stilesville, Bunny Boo!"

Sasha's friends called her 'Bunny Boo' because she was totally into the urban scene, whether it was fashion, music, or attitude!

"Thanks, Jade," Sasha said. She held up a pair of cropped khakis and added, "These are what I'm taking on the trip, though. They're cute too, right?"

"Totally," Cloe agreed.

After the girls had paid for their new outfits, they headed to the sporting goods shop to grab some of the supplies from Miss Couri's list.

"Okay, binoculars, canteens, torches, cameras and sunglasses – anything else we need?" Sasha asked, surveying the items she and her friends had picked out.

"I think that's it," Cloe replied. "I feel totally outdoorsy already!"

"I know, I think we're set," Yasmin agreed. "I can't wait to go on this trip!"

Chapter 3

The next couple of weeks were a whirlwind of packing and preparation, and they totally flew by. Before the girls knew it, spring break had begun, and they were on a plane to the South American rainforest.

On the flight, Jade, Sasha and Fianna sat together in one row, and Cloe, Yasmin and the new girl, Lilee, sat in another. Miss Couri was stuck with the Tweevils in a third.

"Poor Miss Couri!" Jade exclaimed. "I would not be able to take an international flight sitting next to those two."

"I'm sure they'll behave themselves," Sasha replied. "I mean, they're counting on extra credit from her – how annoying can they be?"

"Good point," Fianna agreed.

In the middle row, Kirstee and Kaycee were already bickering.

"Your bag is taking up my foot space," Kaycee whined, swatting at her sister.

"No, your feet are in my personal space," Kirstee complained, batting her twin's hand away.

"Girls, it's a long flight," Miss Couri interrupted, "and we're all in close quarters. Let's try to make the best of it, okay?"

"Yes, Miss Couri," the twins grumbled, folding their hands in their laps obediently. But as soon as their teacher turned away to gaze out the window, they were swatting at each other again.

Meanwhile, in the next row over, Cloe and Yasmin had introduced themselves to the new girl, who seemed really quiet.

"So you just moved here, right?" Cloe asked.

"Yeah," Lilee said softly.

"How do you like Stiles High so far?" Yasmin wanted to know.

"It's okay," Lilee replied. "I'm still getting used to it."

"Yeah, it can definitely be an adjustment," Yasmin agreed. "But I'm sure before long, you'll love it as much as we do!"

"Aren't you so excited about this trip?" Cloe asked. "I mean, how cool is it that we get to explore the rainforest over spring break?"

"Actually, my parents made me sign up," Lilee admitted. "They thought it would be a good way for me to meet new people."

"Well, they were right!" Cloe gushed. "I mean, you've met us already, and our friends Yasmin, Sasha and Fianna are all on this trip too, and they're all totally awesome!"

"Great," Lilee murmured, her eyes lowered. She didn't exactly sound thrilled.

Cloe and Yasmin exchanged a glance, but Yasmin rambled on. "Well, we're in for a long flight, so I'm gonna dig into this cool new novel I brought. Do you girls need any magazines to read? I brought a ton."

"I think I'll just do some sketching," Cloe replied, pulling out her sketchpad.

As the artist of the group, Cloe was constantly drawing, whether she was just doodling or working on a masterpiece.

"Lilee? Magazine?" Yasmin inquired.

"No, I'm okay," Lilee replied. She slipped on her headphones, selected some tunes on her MP3 player, then leaned her head back and closed her eyes.

"Do you think she's okay?" Cloe wrote on her sketchpad. She slipped it over to Yasmin, and Yasmin shrugged, then grabbed Cloe's pencil.

"Just shy," she jotted down. "I'm sure she'll loosen up."

"I hope so!" Cloe wrote back, then quickly flipped to a fresh page so no one else would see their notes.

Miss Couri was already engrossed in a book about the rainforest, while the Tweevils were trying to share a single travel book, both highlighting all the spas and overpriced boutiques they hoped to hit while they were in South America.

Sasha was reading the biography of a big-time female CEO – Sasha had tons of cool role models, but her friends were all sure that she'd be more successful than all of those famous women some day.

Jade took out her portable DVD player and put in one of her favourite comedies. "Feel like a movie?" she asked Fianna.

"Sure!" Fianna agreed. They both plugged their headphones into the DVD player and Jade started the movie. Soon both girls were giggling away.

"Hey, Cloe, you wanna brainstorm some ideas for our magazine?" Yasmin asked a little while later.

"Sounds good," Cloe agreed. She turned to a new page in her sketchpad and started jotting down ideas. "Obviously we're doing a piece on safari fashions."

"Definitely," Yasmin replied. "How about beauty tips for humid climates?"

"Ooh, I could use some of those!" Cloe said. "We should also do something on cool

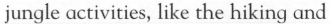

jungle activities, like the hiking and kayaking we'll be doing."

"And we have to include something on how our readers can help save the rainforest," Yasmin added.

"Great idea, Yas!" Cloe exclaimed. "So we should make sure we include a piece on the amazing animals and plants people can find in the rainforest, so

©MGA

they'll see why it's so important to help save them."

"And we could do a travel piece on South America in general, since I'm sure we'll have a totally cool trip there," Yasmin suggested.

"Love it!" Cloe cried. She glanced over her list. "Wow, that's a ton of stuff. We should be pretty much set for this issue, right?"

"I think so," Yasmin told her. "And I'm sure we'll come up with even more ideas once we're there. Now we just need to get to that rainforest so we can really get started!"

Just then the Tweevils walked by, knocking into Cloe and making her scribble all over her list.

"Hey!" Cloe protested.

"Whoopsie!" Kaycee said. "Hope that wasn't important."

Kirstee sneaked a peek at the list on Cloe's tray table. "You weren't plotting out an issue of Bad Magazine, were you?"

"It's called 'Bratz'," Cloe snapped. "And that's none of your business."

"Well, whatever it's called, you're wasting your time," Kirstee replied. "If there's anything worth covering in this musty old jungle, Kaycee and I will be getting the scoop for My Thing Magazine."

Cloe and Yasmin glared at them, but before they could say anything, a flight attendant appeared behind the twins.

"I'm afraid you'll have to return to your seats," she told them. "No loitering in the aisles!"

"Oh darn, and we were having such a nice conversation," Yasmin said. "Well, guess we'll have to catch up with you girls later!"

The Tweevils scurried back to their seats, and Yasmin and Cloe shared a sigh of relief.

"How are we going to survive a whole week with them?" Yasmin whispered once the Tweevils were out of earshot.

"Hey, the rainforest is a big place, right?" Cloe asked. "I'm sure we can totally avoid them."

"I hope you're right," Yasmin replied, turning her attention back to her book. "Because otherwise, those girls could turn this whole amazing trip into a real disaster."

Chapter 4

"We're here!" Jade exclaimed, peering out of her window as they touched down at the edge of a totally lush-looking forest.

"Wow, it looks gorgeous," Sasha murmured.

"Fianna, wake up!" Jade called.

"Wha–?" her friend asked, stirring. "Oh, are we here already?"

"Already?" Sasha cried. "That was, like, the longest flight ever!"

"Well, I got in some good beauty sleep," Fianna replied. "I'm ready to take on the rainforest!"

The eight girls and their teacher filed off the plane and claimed their luggage, then headed out into the sticky afternoon heat.

Their guide, Mr Torres, met them at the curb and helped them load his van with their luggage while Miss Couri made the introductions.

"Mr Torres was my guide on my last trip here," Miss Couri explained. "He knows everything about the rainforest, so he'll be pointing out tons of fantastic plants and animals to you every step of the way."

"Your teacher knows a few things about the rainforest herself," Mr Torres replied, "so I'm sure she'll have plenty to share with you as well."

"We can't wait!" Cloe squealed, hopping into the van. "So what's on the agenda for today?"

"Well, first we'll set up our campsite, and maybe take a little hike around the area to help you start to get a sense of your surroundings," Mr Torres explained. "But I know you're all tired from your flight, so we'll take it easy today."

"And tomorrow, the real adventure begins!" Miss Couri added.

"That's what I like to hear!" Sasha exclaimed.

Mr Torres drove them to a small settlement at the edge of the rainforest.

This is our base camp," he told the girls. "A few of us will hike back here about halfway through our trip to pick up additional supplies. If you've brought more luggage than you can comfortably carry into the jungle, you can also store that here. It's important that you travel light, because we will be on foot for the rest of the way to our camp."

"Why can't we drive, like normal

people?" Kaycee demanded.

"Because the rainforest is far too precious and delicate to plough through it in a huge vehicle," Miss Couri explained. "Going on foot lets us make as little impact on the environment as possible."

"How cool!" Yasmin exclaimed. "I feel like an explorer already!"

She and her friends had packed light, just as Miss Couri had instructed, so they each had only a backpack full of supplies to carry to their campsite. Lilee appeared to have brought hardly anything – her backpack hung limply from her shoulders, and she offered to carry some of their food supplies if Mr Torres needed help with them. The Tweevils, however, were a little more loaded down.

"I have to have my hairdryer!" Kaycee complained as she dug through her suitcases and bags, trying to lighten her load. "And my curling tongs. And my hair straighteners. And–"

"Kaycee, there aren't any electrical outlets in the jungle, so anything you have to plug in can stay here," Miss Couri began.

"Well, I need all of these shoes, and all of these hair products, and – oh, there's nothing here that I can leave behind!" Kirstee moaned.

"We each only brought one pair of shoes," Sasha interrupted. "Just put on the most comfortable ones now and you won't need to carry any extras into the jungle with you."

"Maybe one pair of shoes is enough for you fashion disasters, but I need options," Kirstee snapped. "I mean, not all of my shoes go with all of my outfits."

"Kirstee, everything you own is pink,"

Yasmin pointed out. "It can't be that hard to coordinate."

But Kirstee and Kaycee pretended not to hear. They just kept pulling things out of their bags, making a huge pile of things they had to have and a tiny one of items they could do without.

"And as for hair products – just pull your hair back in a ponytail," Cloe continued, still trying to talk sense into the girls. "I mean, it's not a fashion show – it's a safari!"

"Obviously it's not a fashion show with you losers here!" Kirstee snapped.

"Good one!" Kaycee cried, slapping her sister a high-five.

"Girls, that's enough," Miss Couri declared. "Now I know we're all worn out from that flight, but that's no excuse for rudeness."

She glared at the Tweevils until they

lowered their heads and muttered, "Sorry, Miss Couri."

"If we're going to make it through this week, we have to work together," Miss Couri continued. "We'll have a lot of fun, but there will be a lot of hard work too, and we can't be wasting energy on bickering and other nonsense. Got it?"

All of the girls nodded. "Now, I happen to be an expert packer, so let me take a look here," she told the Tweevils. "Okay, first of all, no skirts or dresses. You can't do any of our safari activities in these."

The Tweevils started to protest, but Miss Couri ignored them.

"No heels. These sneakers will be fine." She pulled out four jackets of varying weights and lengths from the Tweevils' bags, and sighed. "One jacket each will do. Here, tie them around your waist like the other girls did so they aren't taking up room in your backpacks."

As the Tweevils obeyed, Miss Couri kept sorting through their luggage. "Five pairs of trousers will be fine – you don't need ten! Seven shirts, maybe, but not fifteen! Girls, how long did you think we'd be out here?"

"We just wanted to be prepared," Kaycee said softly.

"I appreciate that, but didn't you read the supply list I gave you?" their teacher asked. "I was very specific about how much to pack."

"Those all seemed like low estimates," Kirstee replied. "We pretty much just doubled everything."

"I see that," Miss Couri told her. "But now it's time to halve it. We'll lock everything up in the storage room here at base camp, and you can retrieve it at the end of the week."

"But – what if we run out of clothes?" Kaycee cried desperately.

"We will be picking up supplies here again in a few days," Mr Torres reminded them. "If you need something, you ladies can do the supply run and grab whatever you need."

"Whatever you need that you can also carry back out of the jungle," Miss Couri reminded them.

"Don't we have, like, camels or something that can do that?" Kaycee whined.

"Um, I don't think camels live in the rainforest," Lilee pointed out, speaking up for the first time. Cloe and Yasmin subtly gave each other five behind their backs – it seemed like the new girl had some spirit after all!

"Whatever," Kirstee grumbled.

"Okay, ladies, we need to get moving – we still have a lot of work to do once we reach the campsite," Miss Couri announced.

The girls all picked up their backpacks, while Mr Torres carried most of the supplies. He led them, single-file, down a trail into the jungle, until suddenly Cloe stopped in her tracks.

"Wait, we forgot the tents!" she cried. "What are we gonna do? We'll get sunburned, and attacked by wild monkeys, and–"

"Cloe, it's okay," Mr Torres replied soothingly. "I took a boat to the campsite earlier with the tents and sleeping bags, so they'll be waiting for us when we arrive."

"Whew!" Cloe gasped. Her friends just laughed – Cloe was known for her tendency to be overly dramatic, but she also usually managed to recover quickly.

They resumed their hike and along the way, Mr Torres and Miss Couri pointed out cool animals to them.

"Shh," Mr Torres whispered. "If you look closely, you'll see a howler monkey right there in that tree!"

"Ooh," the girls cooed – all except Kirstee, who shouted, "Where? I don't see it," making the monkey

©MGA

scamper away to a different tree.

"I'm sure you'll see the next one," Mr Torres sighed.

"Girls, check out that giant iguana!" Miss Couri exclaimed, gesturing towards the rainforest floor, where a huge green iguana sat blinking at them, lazily flicking his tongue in and out.

"Cool!" Jade said in an excited whisper. "I've got to grab a picture."

Her camera was slung over her shoulder for easy access, and now she turned it on and snapped a quick close-up of the reptile.

"That's so going in our magazine!" she exclaimed.

"See those exotic orchids?" Miss Couri asked, pointing to some brilliant orange blooms among the foliage.

"Gorgeous!" Cloe cried. She pulled out her camera and took a picture of them. "I'm definitely doing a painting of those when I get home!"

Soon they reached the campsite, where their tents and sleeping bags were all piled on the ground. Mr Torres and Miss Couri led the way into the clearing. Cloe, Jade, Sasha, Yasmin and Fianna were chatting happily while the Tweevils bickered as usual. Lilee trailed behind.

"Okay, decide among yourselves who you want your tentmates to be," Miss Couri told her students. "I'll have my own tent, and Mr Torres will have one to himself, but the rest of you will need to share."

Yasmin noticed Lilee staring at her shoes, certain she wouldn't be picked. Yasmin remembered what it had been like when she was the new girl in school, and hurried over to Lilee to cheer her up.

"Will you share a tent with me?" she asked.

Lilee looked up, startled. "Who – me?" she stammered.

"Yes, you!" Yasmin replied. "Unless you already agreed to share with someone else."

"No – I didn't," Lilee said softly. "I mean, no one else has asked me. So yes, I'd be happy to share a tent with you."

"Good!" Yasmin gave her new friend a big smile, then hurried over to the others to let them know she'd already paired off.

"That was sweet of you, Yas," Cloe told her.

"I just didn't want her to feel left out," Yasmin explained. "And we'll all have plenty of time to hang out on this trip – I figure we'll only be going to our tents to crash."

"Good point," Sasha agreed. "Well, Jade, do you want to share a tent? I am an expert tent-pitcher, so that's one point in

46

my favour."

"Absolutely," Jade declared.

"I guess you're stuck with me," Cloe said to Fianna.

"Okay, as long as I have permission to kick you if you snore," Fianna teased.

"I don't snore – do I?" Cloe gasped. She whirled to face her best friends. "In all our years of sleepovers, how could you not have told me?"

"Angel, I think she was kidding," Jade stage-whispered to her. Cloe's nickname was 'Angel' because of her heavenly, totally dazzling sense of style.

"Right, I knew that," Cloe replied. "So, um…should we put up those tents?"

"Yep – time to make this jungle feel like home!" Sasha announced.

Everyone quickly put up their tents,

except for the Tweevils, who kept getting tangled up in a pile of tent poles and flaps.

"I think we got a broken tent," Kirstee complained.

"I don't think it's the tent," Mr Torres replied as he retrieved them from beneath their tent for the third time.

"But it won't work!" Kaycee moaned.

"Here, let me see if I can fix it?" Mr Torres sighed. He quickly pitched the tent for the twins, and they scurried inside, barely pausing to thank their guide as they pushed past him.

"I don't know how those girls are going to survive in the jungle," Cloe overheard him say to Miss Couri. Cloe stifled a giggle as she ducked back into the tent – the Tweevils and the wilderness definitely seemed like a bad combination.

Chapter 5

"Good morning!" Miss Couri called, peering into each of the girls' tents bright and early the next day. "We've got to get moving – we have some endangered sea turtles to save!"

"Turtles? How cute!" Cloe squealed, suddenly fully awake. She leaned over her friend, who was still curled up in her sleeping bag, and shouted, "Fianna, rise and shine!"

"Five more minutes," Fianna grumbled.

"Fianna, the turtles can't wait!" Cloe insisted.

"Turtles?" Fianna asked. She stretched, slowly coming out of sleep. "Cloe, what are you talking about?"

But Cloe was too busy throwing on her outfit for the day and bounding out of the tent to answer. Fianna trailed out after her moments later, fully dressed but a lot less lively than Cloe. They sat down beside the campfire, where their guide was already preparing breakfast.

"Mmm, that smells great!" Jade cried, emerging from her tent.

"Thank you," Mr Torres replied. "It'll be ready in a minute."

"Can't wait!" Jade replied.

"How'd everyone sleep?" Sasha asked, joining the girls around the campfire.

"Pretty good – you know, considering the hard ground and the creepy rustling

50

sounds in the forest, oh, and of course the heat," Cloe said.

"I didn't hear any rustling sounds," Fianna protested.

"That, my friend, is because you sleep like a log," Cloe declared, slinging her arm around Fianna's shoulder. "Because there were some seriously scary creatures moving in on our camp last night."

"There's really nothing to be afraid of here," Mr Torres insisted. "Of course we're surrounded by a lot of wildlife, but I've never had an animal disturb the camp."

Yasmin joined them just in time to hear this exchange.

"Don't mind Cloe," she told their guide. "She's easily freaked out."

"What's that supposed to mean?" Cloe cried. Her friends stared her down until she admitted, "okay, it's true, I'm easily freaked out. Sorry, Mr Torres – I didn't mean to question your guiding abilities."

"No problem," Mr Torres replied. "The jungle can take some getting used to. But I'm sure that soon you'll love it as much as I do!"

He stirred the eggs one more time, then announced, "Breakfast time!"

"Hey, where's Lilee?" Jade asked Yasmin.

"Still in the tent," Yasmin replied. "But I'm sure she'll be up for food. I'll go and get her." She strolled back towards her tent, but on her way noticed Miss Couri still trying to rouse the Tweevils from their tent.

"Need some help?" Yasmin asked her teacher.

"I've never seen anything like it," Miss Couri replied. "It's like they can't even hear me."

"I'll take care of it," Yasmin promised.

She ducked into the tent and called, "Hey, Kirstee, thanks for letting me borrow your pink jacket!"

"What? No!" Kirstee cried, leaping out of her sleeping bag. "I do not want Bratz cooties on my new jacket. Kaycee, wake up!" She shook her sister awake and continued, "Yasmin's trying to steal my jacket!"

"Save your own jacket," Kaycee complained. "I'm trying to get some beauty sleep."

"Keep sleeping if you want to, but then we'll have to eat all the food without you," Yasmin replied with a shrug.

"Oh no, we'll starve!" Kaycee exclaimed. "Kirstee, we have to get out there before those Bratz eat everything!"

The Tweevils pushed past Yasmin and Miss Couri and made a dash for the campfire.

"Thanks," Miss Couri said, trying to hide her laughter.

"Happy to help," Yasmin replied. She headed over to her tent and leaned in. "Lilee, are you ready for some breakfast?"

"Sure," Lilee agreed. "I'll be right there."

Once they were all gathered around the campfire and munching on the tasty breakfast Mr Torres had made, Miss Couri explained that they would be taking a nature hike to a nearby beach that was home to four species of endangered turtles.

"We need to help clean up their beach, make sure their nests are safe and help release hatched baby turtles into the ocean," Miss Couri continued. "Is everyone up for that?"

"Sounds awesome!" Yasmin squealed.

"Glad to hear it," Miss Couri said with a grin. "Well, finish up your breakfasts, get into your hiking clothes and then we'll hit the trail."

They hiked beneath the arching leaves of giant palm trees. Along the way, they spotted brightly coloured macaws, a cute tiny tree frog and a funny animal called a capybara that looked like a giant guinea pig.

"The animals here are incredible!" Jade exclaimed.

"Wait till you see these turtles," Miss Couri told her.

Suddenly, they burst out of the forest and found themselves at the edge of the bright-blue ocean, on a beach dotted with giant sea turtles.

"Wow!" Sasha cried. "This is where we'll be working all day?"

"Not bad, right?" Mr Torres asked.

"Yeah, I think I can handle this,"

Fianna agreed happily.

They were met by a scientist named Ms Soto, who ran the turtle hatchery on the beach.

"The hatchery is here to protect the turtles' nests, make sure their eggs hatch and then get the baby turtles safely back to the ocean," she explained. "Today, you'll be helping us with all of that."

She showed them how to move the turtles' nests to the hatchery without disturbing the eggs and how to carry the tiny, adorable baby turtles safely to be released into the ocean again.

"They're so sweet," Cloe cooed.

Jade snapped a picture of her best friend with a baby sea turtle, and Cloe took a group shot of her friends with a giant turtle.

"I'm crazy about that shell pattern," Jade told her friends, gazing in amazement at the

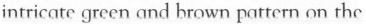

intricate green and brown pattern on the turtle's shell. "I'm totally designing a dress based on it when we get home!"

"Kool Kat, that is such a cool idea!" Sasha exclaimed. Jade's friends called her 'Kool Kat' because she was always on the cutting edge of the latest trends.

Kirstee and Kaycee were assigned to clean up the beach while the others took care of the turtles.

"Why can't I have a baby

turtle?" Kaycee whined. "Those Bratz get all the baby turtles they want!"

"Duh, Kaycee," her sister sighed, "they aren't keeping the turtles. They're, like, releasing them into the wild."

"I wanna release turtles into the wild," Kaycee complained.

"You do not," Kirstee snapped.

"Oh," Kaycee replied, and continued cleaning up the beach in silence.

The girls spent all day helping out at the beach, and even the Tweevils seemed to be enjoying it by the end. Although Lilee kept pretty much to herself all day, Yasmin noticed that she was really gentle with the turtles and seemed totally happy to be helping them.

"She's such a sweet girl," Yasmin said to her friends. "I just wish I could find a way to bring her out of her shell."

"Ha! Shell!" Jade exclaimed.

"That was not a turtle joke," Yasmin told her.

"Oh, come on," Jade insisted. "It totally was!"

"Whatever, I really want to find a way to help her," Yasmin insisted.

"Pretty Princess, you've helped her a ton already," Jade replied. Yasmin was known as 'Pretty Princess' because of her totally glamorous, almost regal style. "Don't worry – I'm sure she'll loosen up."

"You all did a fantastic job," Ms Soto announced, when it was time to go. "The turtles and I truly appreciate all your hard work."

"Helping these amazing animals didn't feel like work," Sasha gushed.

"Glad you enjoyed it," Miss Couri said

as she and Mr Torres led the students back into the jungle.

All the way back to camp, the girls talked excitedly about the sea turtles. "It was awesome getting to hold those baby turtles!" Fianna exclaimed.

"I know, and I feel like we totally helped them," Yasmin added.

"You did," Miss Couri interjected.

When they reached the camp, Miss Couri offered to take them swimming at a nearby waterfall. The girls all hurried into their tents and changed into their swimsuits, then followed Miss Couri. Mr Torres headed off into the jungle alone while the girls and their teacher went swimming.

The waterfall splashed over a cliff into a clear blue pool and was totally breathtaking. The girls leapt into the chilly water and splashed around, giggling and snapping tons of photos with Sasha's waterproof camera.

Even Miss Couri joined in the fun, doing a cannonball into the water and floating on her back in the placid pool.

The Tweevils refused to even dip a toe in the water, choosing to sunbathe instead in their ridiculous matching pink ruffled swimsuits.

"Who knows what could be in there?" Kaycee wailed.

"Well, if we find anything scary, we'll let you know," Jade told her.

Lilee sat by herself at the edge of the pool, and although the girls encouraged her to get in the water, she merely shook her head.

"This'll be perfect for our tropical swimwear feature," Jade declared, striking a pose in her tiger-print swimsuit as Sasha took her picture.

"Ooh, count me in!" Cloe exclaimed, doing a twirl in her camouflage-print suit. "Hey, Fianna, come and be in a picture with me!" Fianna strutted over in her leaf-patterned bikini, and the girls posed for a photo.

"I'm totally tropical," Yasmin added, doing a quick catwalk strut alongside the pool in her hibiscus-patterned one-piece. "Sasha, you can get in on the action too, with that bright orange tankini."

She pulled her friend out of the water and Jade snapped a shot with Sasha's camera.

"These aren't really going in the magazine, though, are they?" Yasmin asked. "I was making the silliest face in that one!"

"We'll just have to see, won't we?" Jade

teased, making them all crack up.

They were all having such a great time that no one noticed when Lilee silently slipped away.

Chapter 6

"Oh my gosh, what happened to our campsite?" Cloe wailed when they returned from the waterfall to find all their tents crumpled into messy piles.

"Oh no, where's Lilee?" Miss Couri cried, looking around frantically. "Lilee, are you okay?"

Just then, the new girl emerged from the woods.

"I'm right here," Lilee said. "I just went for a walk while you were at the waterfall. I'm sorry, I should have told you where I was going."

"Yes, you should have," Miss Couri declared. "Girls, you absolutely cannot go wandering off in the jungle alone, do you understand me?"

"Yes, Miss Couri," they all chorused.

Lilee looked totally embarrassed, so Yasmin went over to make sure she was okay.

"Weren't you having fun at the waterfall?" she inquired.

"I don't know – I guess I just got bored," Lilee replied.

Sasha joined them and asked, "You know you can always hang with us, right? I mean, I know we

get caught up in our own thing sometimes, but you can totally join in if you want."

"Oh – thanks," Lilee murmured. "But I just really felt like going for a walk, that's all."

"Well, next time you want to go for a walk, just ask one of us to go too," Jade insisted. "We've got to stick together, okay?!"

"Okay, that's really sweet and all, but what are we gonna do about our campsite?" Kirstee demanded.

"Yeah – it's like, totally ruined!" Kaycee cried.

"For once, I have to agree with Kaycee and Kirstee," Cloe admitted. "We have to fix this, and fast!"

The sun had already gone down, and the girls, their teacher and their guide struggled to put the tents up again in the dark. They were up half the night and finally collapsed, exhausted, into their sleeping bags just a few hours before dawn.

"What do you think happened to our tents, anyway?" Sasha asked the next morning. She and her friends were huddled around the campfire, yawning and barely able to keep their eyes open.

"Do you think the Tweevils had something to do with it?" Cloe wondered.

"No way," Jade replied. "They suffered at least as much as we did last night. And they would never do anything that would inconvenience them."

"True," Yasmin agreed. "It was probably just the wind or something."

"Yeah, or a marauding animal!" Cloe cried.

"I'm sure it was the wind," Yasmin insisted.

Lilee wandered out of her tent and sat down on the opposite side of the campfire. Soon the Tweevils dragged themselves out of their tent, too.

"So, today we'll be kayaking down the river," Miss Couri announced once the girls had all gathered around.

"Awesome!" Sasha exclaimed.

"It should be a ton of fun," Miss Couri agreed. "Let's get moving!"

The group hiked to the mouth of the river, where five river kayaks were waiting for them.

"Kirstee, I want you to ride with me, and Kaycee, you'll ride with Mr Torres," Miss Couri said. "The rest of you can pick your own kayak partners."

"Are we in trouble?" Kaycee asked.

"No – we wanted extra-special help from you and your sister," Miss Couri explained.

Cloe and Jade exchanged a glance, sure that their teacher was just worried that the twins would shove each other out of their kayak if they rode together. Cloe asked Lilee to ride with her, while Jade paired with Fianna and Sasha went with Yasmin.

Mr Torres showed them all how to paddle, then helped them launch their kayaks into the river.

"Whoa, we're totally flying!" Jade exclaimed as they cruised down the river.

"Check out the view!" Fianna added, gazing up at the jungle above them, which trailed down the cliff face towards the riverbank.

"I love it here," Jade agreed.

Yasmin was busily jotting down notes in between paddles, explaining to Sasha, "This has got to be our cover story. What an incredible adventure!"

"Ooh, we should do a piece on wilderness workouts, too," Sasha added. "'cause this is a serious workout, right here!"

Cloe kept trying to start a conversation with Lilee, but the new girl refused to say more than a few words at a time.

"Is everything okay?" Cloe asked finally.

"What?" Lilee had been staring up at the trees, but now glanced back at Cloe, who sat behind her in the boat. "Oh – yeah. I guess I'm just not really a safari person, you know?"

"But you were great with those turtles yesterday," Cloe insisted. "And besides, it's so beautiful here – how can you not love it?"

Lilee paused for a long time, and Cloe thought she wasn't going to answer. But finally, Lilee agreed, "It is pretty amazing."

Cloe felt like she was finally starting to

get through to the new girl, but they were interrupted when Kaycee ran her kayak into the riverbank. They all pulled their kayaks onto a nearby sandbar and walked back to help dig out Kaycee and poor Mr Torres.

As soon as they were free, Kirstee managed to tip over her kayak, dumping poor Miss Couri in the river along with her. Sasha and Yasmin helped fish her out, while Jade and Fianna retrieved their boat and flipped it back over for them.

While they were helping Miss Couri and Kirstee back into their kayak, they spotted a group of pink-toned dolphins swimming playfully.

"Whoa, I didn't know dolphins could live in rivers!" Fianna exclaimed.

"They do in South America,"

©MGA

Miss Couri explained as she settled herself into her boat. "So this is the place to see them!"

"Wow," Jade sighed, watching the dolphins frolic down the river. "There sure are a lot of incredible animals in the rainforest."

"That's why I wanted to bring you guys here," Miss Couri replied, "so you could check out the amazing diversity of species."

"Maybe that's a good high point to end our kayak trip on," Mr Torres suggested, brushing leaves out of his hair, left over from his crash-landing with Kaycee.

They all turned their kayaks around and headed back to the bank, paddling hard to make it upstream. Jade paused to wave goodbye to the dolphins as they paddled away.

"Sorry we had to cut the trip short,"

Miss Couri said when they returned to their campsite. She had changed into dry clothes right away and now was towelling off her hair.

"Don't worry about it," Yasmin replied. "It was still amazing."

"And anyway, we're all still beat from the tent trouble last night," Sasha added. "It'll be good to hit the sack early tonight."

"Actually, would it be okay if we took a nap before dinner?" Jade asked.

"Good idea," Miss Couri agreed. They all headed to their tents to rest.

A little later, everyone was awakened by the Tweevils' piercing screams.

"What happened? What happened?" Miss Couri cried, bolting out of her tent.

"Our food! It's all gone!" Kaycee wailed.

Their supplies were scattered all over their campsite, and every edible scrap had been devoured.

"What did you two do?" Sasha demanded, joining the others in the clearing.

"Nothing!" Kirstee protested. "We woke up and wanted a snack, but all we found was this!"

"This is terrible," Mr Torres declared. "It's too late to head to base camp now – we'll have to hike there in the morning and restock."

"Ooh, good, then I can get my other pink outfit!" Kaycee squealed.

"What a relief," Mr Torres replied dryly. "Well, for now, we'd better all get back to bed."

"You mean, without any supper?" Kirstee whined.

"We don't exactly have a choice," Jade pointed out.

"Fine. But if I find out it was you Bratz, I will get you," Kirstee vowed.

"She's not kidding," Kaycee whispered after her sister stalked away. "She takes her dinner very seriously."

With that, she scurried after her twin.

"Guess I'll go to bed too," Lilee murmured, and trudged back to her tent.

"How do you think this happened?" Yasmin wondered.

"It was probably just wild animals," Sasha replied.

"But we saw Mr Torres secure all the food in the trees, where the animals couldn't reach it," Fianna pointed out. "I mean, he knows what he's doing. This is his job."

"Maybe the Tweevils were pigging out

and got carried away," Cloe suggested.

"I don't think so," Jade said. "They seemed really upset, and they aren't exactly good actresses."

"Well, who do you think did it, then?" Yasmin asked.

"I don't know yet," Jade replied. "But I think there's something seriously strange going on here. And we'd better get to the bottom of it."

Chapter 7

In the morning, Mr Torres led the Tweevils back to base camp to pick up food and more pink clothing, while Miss Couri took the others on a nature hike near their campsite. They saw toucans and anteaters, and Lilee even saw a jaguar making its way through the underbrush.

"Well spotted, Lilee!" Miss Couri cried. "The jaguar is one of the rainforest's most magnificent animals – and one of the most endangered ones, too. We're very lucky to have seen one."

Mr Torres and the Tweevils were gone for a long time, and by the time they got back from base camp, it was time to have dinner and then go to bed.

"What took so long?" Miss Couri asked, after the Tweevils and Lilee had gone to their tents.

"Wardrobe dilemma," Mr Torres sighed. "And some disagreements about who was walking too close to whom."

"Sounds awful," Miss Couri replied. "Sorry you had to deal with them."

"I've seen worse," Mr Torres told her.

"Seriously?" she asked, amazed.

"Actually, yes," he said, laughing.

After the adults said goodnight, the girls sat around the campfire working on articles for their magazine. Yasmin wrote about their sea-turtle rescue, Jade focused on safari fashions, Cloe jotted down notes about the cool creatures they'd seen on their hikes so far, Sasha wrote about their kayaking trip, and Fianna came up with beauty tips.

"This is going to be the best issue of Bratz Magazine ever!" Cloe declared.

"We should do travel issues more often," Yasmin suggested. "I mean, there are so many awesome places we could go, and so many more amazing things we could write about."

"Now, if only we could get Miss Couri to take us on a world tour," Jade teased.

"Hey, girls, we'd better get to bed," Sasha said, checking the time on her sports watch. "I'm sure we'll have an early morning again tomorrow."

"Let's just hope we can get through tomorrow without any more disasters," Cloe sighed.

"Sounds good to me," Fianna agreed. "Two disasters are about my limit for any trip."

The girls all said goodnight, and Yasmin slipped quietly into her tent, careful not to wake Lilee. But Yasmin was so tired that she didn't notice that Lilee was still lying awake in her sleeping bag, waiting for her tentmate to return.

By the next morning, everything was looking sunnier. The day was clear and hot, and the girls were eager for their next rainforest adventure.

Over breakfast, Yasmin had another story idea for their magazine – fun campfire recipes. She stopped by her tent to jot down her idea, and discovered that all of their articles and notes from the entire trip were missing.

"You guys, we have a situation here," she told her best friends, pulling them aside.

"Yas, what happened?" Sasha asked worriedly.

"Our notes are gone," Yasmin told them. "All of them."

"Wait, so all the work we've done on our stories for this entire trip has been a total waste?" Cloe wailed.

"Well...we can probably recreate them," Yasmin reassured her friend.

"Or we could figure out who took them, and get them back," Jade declared.

"It has to be the Tweevils," Sasha said. "They were desperate to get the scoop for Your Thing Magazine, and with our notes gone, they've got it."

"Okay, that's it. We're watching those twins 24-7 until we catch them in the act," Jade told her friends.

"I'm on it," Cloe agreed.

"They won't get away with this," Sasha added.

"And we will get those notes back!" Yasmin cried.

That day, the whole group went mountain climbing up the side of a dormant volcano, now covered in the same lush greenery as the rest of the rainforest.

"I can't believe I'm actually walking on a volcano!" Cloe exclaimed.

"I know, isn't it amazing?" Miss Couri asked. "I love it up here, overlooking the entire rainforest. I think you really get a sense of how vast and magnificent it is."

"Totally," Fianna agreed.

"Ooh, girls, there's a tapir!" Miss Couri cried, pointing through the foliage to a squat black creature with a floppy nose.

"Where?" Kaycee shrieked, clutching her sister's arm. "I can't stand tapirs!"

"Kaycee, are you sure you know what a tapir is?" Miss Couri asked.

"Well…no," Kaycee admitted. "But they sound scary."

"They aren't," Miss Couri promised. "They're related to rhinoceroses, but they look like a cross between a pig and an anteater. Now how scary can that be?"

"I don't know…" Kaycee replied. "I don't really like pigs or anteaters."

Miss Couri just sighed. A little further along the trail, Kirstee shrieked, "It's got me! Something's got me!"

Miss Couri rushed to her side and discovered that Kirstee's shirt had snagged on a branch, while a leaf had brushed against her face, convincing the girl that she was under attack.

"It's just a tree," Miss Couri explained. "It can't hurt you."

"Are you sure it isn't a killer tree?" Kirstee demanded. "Because I've heard of weird killer plants in places like this, and if I'm poisoned or something, I need to know now."

"Kirstee, you're fine," Miss Couri insisted. "Now, I have to get back to the head of the trail so no one gets lost."

With that, she strode briskly away.

"If I didn't know better, I'd think our teacher was trying to escape from the Tweevils," Fianna whispered.

"I know!" Cloe exclaimed. "But really, wouldn't you?"

"Seriously, though, the Tweevils seem scared of everything out here," Jade said. "I think they're so freaked out that they wouldn't have the energy to mess with us even if they wanted to."

"I know – they've hardly said a mean thing to us in days," Cloe added. "It's kind of weirding me out."

"They did say they needed that Biology extra credit," Sasha reminded her friends. "Maybe they really are on their best behaviour."

"Maybe," Yasmin agreed uncertainly as they continued up the side of the volcano. "Whoa!" she yelled, as they reached the crest and saw the rainforest spread out all around them, green and gorgeous and thriving. She wondered how anyone could dream of destroying such a vibrant place.

The calls of monkeys and tropical birds echoed from branch to branch, creating a constant soundtrack that followed the girls every step of the way.

"How could they not love it here?" Yasmin murmured, soaking in the view and feeling totally tranquil.

"Nature isn't for everyone," Cloe replied with a shrug as they began their trek back down.

When they reached their camp that night, the whole group ate a dinner of delicious empanadas together, and then everyone went to bed. But when they were sure everyone else was asleep, the five friends sneaked back to the campfire to discuss their situation. Yasmin didn't notice that her tentmate followed her back towards the campfire, hanging back in the shadows so the girls wouldn't see her.

"If it's not the Tweevils, who could it be?" Fianna asked.

"Well, it's definitely not Miss Couri," Cloe said. Then she gasped, her eyes going wide with shock. "What if it's Mr Torres? I mean, think about it – none of us knows anything about him, and he's supposed to be in charge of keeping this trip running smoothly – and it has definitely not run smoothly."

"But why would he want to sabotage our trip?" Yasmin asked. "This is how he makes his living – why would he throw all that away?"

"He is really mysterious, though," Jade pointed out. "Always going off by himself, and not telling anyone where he's going or where he's been. And he didn't seem shocked by any of the things that went wrong."

"That's true!" Cloe cried. "Maybe he's secretly sick of all of us tourists trekking through his jungle and messing it up."

"Or maybe having to share a kayak with Kaycee and go on a private hike with both Tweevils drove him over the edge," Fianna added.

"I know that would drive me over the edge," Jade agreed.

"Okay, so how do we find out if he's the culprit?" Yasmin asked.

"I say we just walk right up to him and demand to know the truth," Sasha declared.

"But we need him to guide us back out of the jungle," Cloe pointed out. "If we accuse him, he might leave us here forever! And I like the rainforest, but I don't want to stay here forever!"

"Cloe, he's not going to abandon us in the jungle," Sasha said sensibly. "And besides, Miss Couri knows her way around the rainforest, too. I'm sure we'd manage, even without Mr Torres."

"I hope we won't have to," Jade replied. "But I just don't know who else it could be. And if it is him, I really don't want to be following him through the jungle any more!"

"So what's the plan?" Fianna wanted to know.

"We'll wait for him to sneak off tomorrow, and then we'll follow him and catch him in the act," Jade announced. "Then we'll confront him, all together, and make him confess. It won't be easy, but it has to be done."

Her friends nodded in grim agreement.

Lilee sneaked back into her tent while the other girls were saying their goodnights and lay awake on her sleeping bag, staring up into the darkness and feeling incredibly guilty. She knew none of the things that had happened were Mr Torres' fault, but she was terrified of telling these girls who the real culprit was. She tossed and turned all night. By morning, the only thing she had decided was that when the girls followed Mr Torres, she would have to follow them.

Chapter 8

The girls got up earlier than usual the next morning, and caught Mr Torres just as he was slipping out of his tent and sneaking off into the jungle.

"Follow that guide!" Jade cried.

They tracked Mr Torres through the rainforest until he reached a clearing. There, they hid behind a fringe of trees, watching as he prowled around the clearing, looking very suspicious.

The girls didn't notice someone else following them, hiding further back in the jungle and spying on them while they spied on Mr Torres.

"What is he doing?" Fianna whispered.

"I don't know, but I bet it's not good!" Cloe declared. "Let's get him!"

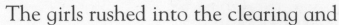

The girls rushed into the clearing and Jade cried, "Stop right there!"

Mr Torres jumped at the sound of her voice.

"Um, hi, girls. What are you doing here?" he asked, looking confused.

"We could ask you the same thing," Sasha said coldly.

"Well, I'm scouting out a clearing that we'll probably work on replanting today," he explained.

©MGA

"You see, this isn't supposed to be a clearing at all – it was illegally cut down – and, as part of your volunteer work here, you'll be helping to revive the forest by planting new trees here."

"But why'd you have to sneak away to do that?" Jade demanded.

"I'm your guide, so it's my job to scout ahead," he explained. "I always get up before my tour group to check out the areas we'll be exploring that day. Why, what did you think I was doing?"

"Wait, so you're saying that every time you sneaked off, you were just doing your job?" Cloe asked.

"Of course," Mr Torres replied. "What else would I be doing? Now, would you girls mind telling me what's going on here?"

"It's just that so many strange things have been happening on this trip," Yasmin

93

explained. "First our tents got knocked down, then all our food got destroyed, and then our notes got stolen."

"What notes?" Mr Torres asked. "I didn't hear anything about that."

"We were planning to do a special rainforest issue of our magazine," Jade explained. "We thought it would be a great way to raise awareness of what an awesome place this is. But now all our notes are gone, and I don't know how we'll ever write our stories without them!"

"I would love to see a magazine all about this magnificent rainforest," Mr Torres said.

"But I thought you were tired of having outsiders tramping through your jungle all the time," Cloe said.

Mr Torres looked shocked, then replied slowly, "First of all, it's not 'my' jungle. It's a natural wonder, and I think everyone should get the opportunity to discover its beauty. That's why I love what I do. And it is my job to guide people through the rainforest. Why would I have a problem with doing my job?"

"I guess that really doesn't make sense," Jade admitted. "But if you weren't sabotaging our trip, who was?"

"Well, I didn't want to say anything until I was sure, but…" Their guide looked from one girl to the other, took a deep breath and continued, "Well, I followed your friend Lilee back from the waterfall and saw her messing around with the tents. I know I should have mentioned something then, but she seemed like such a sweet girl, and I didn't want to get her in trouble. Then I woke up early from my nap the day that the food disappeared, and I did see her taking it down from the tree – but I thought she was just getting a snack."

"It's been her all along," Jade gasped. "It makes sense, Yas – she had the easiest access to our notes, too, since she was sleeping right there in your tent."

The girl who had been hiding in the trees behind them clapped her hand over her mouth in horror. She had planned to tell them the truth as soon as they approached Mr Torres, but then she got scared and now she was afraid it was too late.

"But she seems so sweet!" Yasmin protested. "How could she do something like that?"

"Well, we really don't know her that well," Sasha pointed out.

"And she has pretty much stayed away from us this whole trip, even though we keep trying to make friends with her," Cloe added.

"I just can't believe it," Yasmin insisted. "She's just shy – I can't believe she'd do anything that mean."

"Well, we'll just have to find out for ourselves," Jade replied. "We'll ask her about it while we're all planting trees today."

When Lilee heard this, she ran back to the campsite so she could think in her tent, alone, for a little while, about how to respond when they questioned her.

"Thanks for the tip, Mr Torres," Fianna said. "And sorry we suspected you."

"It's okay," their guide replied. "I know you were just trying to figure out what was going on."

"But you've been

9

such a helpful guide," Cloe told him. "I feel terrible that we accused you."

"We all do," Sasha added. "How can we make it up to you?"

"Find those notes and put out your rainforest issue," Mr Torres replied. "I think it could really make a difference, and it would mean a lot to me to know that one of my tours helped inspire it."

"Ooh, we can write all about what an awesome guide you are, too!" Cloe cried.

"Hey, I wouldn't have a problem with that," their guide said with a grin.

The girls followed their guide back to the campsite, where everyone else was now awake.

"Where were you?" Miss Couri asked the girls. "Didn't I tell you not to wander off?"

"They didn't," Mr Torres interrupted. "I took them on an early-morning nature hike.

I hope you don't mind."

"Oh – well, as long as you were with them, I guess it's okay," Miss Couri replied uncertainly.

"So, what's on the agenda for today?" Fianna asked.

"Please tell me we're taking it easy today," Kirstee begged.

"Yeah – this is supposed to be a holiday, and I haven't got to sleep in on one single day!" Kaycee complained.

"Actually, today is the most important day of our trip so far," Miss Couri announced. "We'll be replacing trees that people have cut down, and really helping to save the rainforest by literally creating more rainforest. Do you girls think you can manage that?"

"I guess so," the Tweevils muttered.

"You guess so?" Yasmin exclaimed. "Oh

come on! What could be more exciting than helping to preserve one of the most spectacular resources on the planet?"

The Tweevils rolled their eyes, but stopped complaining.

They all headed to the clearing with their backpacks full of seeds. Miss Couri explained how deep to plant the seeds and how far apart they should be, and the girls got to work.

Yasmin staked out a spot on one side of Lilee, and Jade began planting on her other side. Cloe, Sasha and Fianna picked nearby spots, too. They had agreed that Yasmin would start the conversation, since she knew Lilee a little better than the others did.

They worked in silence for a while, until Yasmin finally began, "So, Lilee, I have something to ask you."

"Okay," Lilee said cautiously.

"Well, I'm sure you've noticed that some strange things have happened on this trip," Yasmin continued.

"You mean like Kaycee and Kirstee's unlimited supply of pink clothing?" Lilee asked, making Yasmin laugh.

"You're right, that is strange," Yasmin agreed. "But that's not exactly what I meant."

"Oh. You mean the tents, and the food," Lilee said.

"Well – yeah," Yasmin replied. "And our notes on this trip for our next magazine issue just disappeared, too."

"At first we thought the problems were just accidents," Jade chimed in. "But taking our notes couldn't have been an accident."

Lilee had stopped planting and just sat on the ground, staring at her hands, which were clenched in her lap. After a moment, she looked up and whispered, "Actually, that was an accident."

"What?" Yasmin cried, thinking she couldn't have heard right. "How would you know that?"

"Because I did it," Lilee admitted.

Chapter 9

"What?!" Yasmin and her friends all exclaimed.

"How could you?" Yasmin demanded. "I thought we were friends!"

"I wanted to be friends," Lilee replied. "I mean, you and your friends were so nice to me, but you all know each other so well that I didn't know how to join in."

"Oh, we didn't mean to make you feel left out!" Cloe cried.

"I know you didn't," Lilee told her. "But… well…I've never had a tight group of friends like you girls. So I wasn't sure how to act."

"So you stole our stuff?" Sasha snapped.

"No!" Lilee protested. "That's not how it happened."

"Let her explain," Yasmin insisted. Turning to Lilee, she added, "Go on."

"Thanks, Yasmin," Lilee replied meekly. "Okay, so I was trying to think of ways to make you like me–"

"You didn't have to make us like you!" Yasmin interrupted.

"I know," Lilee said. "But still, I wanted to do something nice. It all started with the tents."

"How was wrecking our tents nice?" Jade demanded.

"Jade!" Yasmin hissed.

"Sorry," Jade murmured.

"When we were all changing into our swimsuits, I heard you girls complaining about how hot it was in the tents," Lilee continued. "So I came back early from the waterfall so I could move them to the shade. I figured everyone would be happy and, well – I'd have saved the day."

"So what happened?" Cloe asked.

"I couldn't move the tents all by myself," Lilee admitted. "I kept trying, but I ended up knocking them all over, and I couldn't get them back up. Then I felt so terrible for keeping everyone up all night fixing them that I decided I'd cook everyone a really nice dinner to make up for it."

"That's really sweet," Fianna interjected.

"See, cooking is my speciality," Lilee explained. "It's, like, the one thing I'm really good at."

"Oh, come on, I'm sure you're good at other things too!" Yasmin interrupted.

"Well, not pitching tents, apparently," Lilee replied, cracking a smile.

"So what happened with your dinner?" Jade asked.

"I laid out all the food while everyone was napping, and then I went to gather some firewood," Lilee told them. "When I got back, the food was all ripped to shreds, just the way you saw it. I was only gone for a few minutes, but some animal must have got to it while I was gone."

"That's awful!" Cloe exclaimed.

"Well, I felt awful, anyway," Lilee said. "I know it was stupid of me to leave all the food out like that, and I was so upset that I couldn't stand to tell anyone what I'd done."

"We all make mistakes," Sasha replied.

"Even you, Sasha?" Jade gasped, grinning at her friend.

"Even me," Sasha agreed. "Sometimes." She turned back to Lilee and continued, "I totally understand what happened with the tents and the food. But what's the deal with our notes?"

"I kept hearing you girls talking about all those awesome articles you were writing," Lilee explained. "I know I shouldn't have been eavesdropping but, well – I didn't have anyone to talk to, and you guys were always having such interesting conversations."

"You could've talked to us!" Cloe insisted.

"I know that now," Lilee answered. "But

I just didn't feel confident enough to jump in before, you know?"

"I can understand that," Yasmin replied. "It's not easy when you're the only newcomer to a whole group of people."

"Anyway, I really wanted to read those articles," Lilee said. "And I know I should've just asked, but every time I tried, I got totally nervous. And then I saw them just sitting in our tent and, well – I grabbed them."

"Lilee," Sasha sighed, shaking her head.

"I know, I feel terrible!" Lilee cried. "It's bad enough that I took them, but then I was reading them over the campfire, and the fire was dying down so I had to

©MGA

lean in close to keep reading and – well – I dropped all your notes in the fire. I tried to get them out, I really did, but they burned so fast…"

"So our stories are gone forever?" Cloe moaned.

"Yeah," Lilee admitted. "I'm so, so sorry. Especially because those articles were fantastic! I know they would have made an incredible issue of your magazine. I feel so bad that no one else will ever get to read them."

"Well, I'm glad you liked them," Yasmin said sadly.

"I wanted to tell you sooner, I really did," Lilee said pleadingly. "I never meant for Mr Torres to get wrapped up in this!"

"How do you know about that?" Jade asked.

"I–I overheard you at the campfire last

night, so I decided to follow you this morning," Lilee explained. "If you hadn't believed Mr Torres, I would have jumped in right away and told you it was me all along. But you did, and then he accused me, and I got so scared that I just ran back to camp. So I'm sorry for that, too."

"You can't just spy on people!" Sasha blurted out.

"But I wasn't, really," Lilee insisted. "I was just trying to find a way to tell you the truth. But sometimes it's hard for me to say the right thing at the right time."

"Hey, how come they get to stop planting?" Kirstee complained, stalking over to the six girls who were crouched together on the ground, deep in conversation.

"Yeah, do we get a break too?" Kaycee demanded.

"Girls, what's going on here?" Miss

Couri asked, following the Tweevils across the clearing. "I thought you wanted to help save the rainforest."

"We do," Cloe replied. "But Lilee was just explaining how she accidentally knocked down the tents, and left all the food out, and dropped our notes on the rainforest into the campfire."

"What?" Kirstee cried. "You messed up our tents and lost all our food?"

"But why?" Kaycee wailed.

"It was an accident," Sasha snapped. "Actually, a whole series of accidents."

"Lilee, is this true?" Miss Couri asked.

Lilee nodded, her eyes filling with tears. "I was just trying to help. But everything I tried was a total disaster."

"Hey, I think everything you tried to do was really nice," Yasmin said, putting her arm around Lilee comfortingly. Lilee had made some mistakes, but Yasmin knew she was a good person, and she wasn't going to just stand by and let the new girl feel miserable. "And sure, things didn't work out exactly like you'd planned – but that's just because you tried to do everything by yourself."

"If you'd just asked us, we could have made it a lot easier to put your awesome plans into action," Sasha added. "I mean, it's always easier to do something when you have other people to help you!"

"I know, after we finish planting here, why don't we try all the things you wanted to do?" Jade suggested. "Then we could fix everything, just like you planned. After all, everyone deserves a second chance."

"Yeah!" the girls chorused.

"Miss Couri, you aren't mad at Lilee, are you?" Cloe asked anxiously.

"No – I think I understand what happened," their teacher replied. "And I think it's really great of you girls to help Lilee put everything right."

"Hey, I'm still mad about our food," Kaycee whined.

"Kaycee, you have to let it go," Fianna told her.

"But–" Kaycee began, but Miss Couri interrupted.

"Back to your planting, ladies!" she called. "The sooner you get those seeds in the ground, the sooner the rainforest can start replenishing itself!"

"And the sooner we can go lie down in our tents," Kirstee added under her breath.

Chapter 10

"Lilee, you were right!" Fianna exclaimed, checking out their tents' new arrangement. "We should totally have put them in the shade in the first place!"

Everyone, even the Tweevils, had worked together to move the tents, and with so many people helping, it had been really easy to do. And it was definitely much cooler – and more comfortable – in the shade.

Lilee was eager to make them all dinner that night – she knew cooking was her opportunity to shine. Her new friends helped her chop ingredients and boil water, but she insisted on doing the actual cooking herself so the meal would be a total surprise.

After she set a plate of fabulous-looking

pasta in front of each of her trailmates, Lilee asked nervously, "Well? How is it?"

She seemed to be bracing herself, expecting the worst.

"Lilee, this is delicious!" Cloe exclaimed. "I can't believe you made this over a campfire!"

"Totally amazing!" Jade agreed. "Imagine what you could do with an actual stove!"

©MGA

"Best dinner ever!" Sasha added. "No offence, Mr Torres."

"No, I agree – this is better than anything I've ever made!" Mr Torres replied.

"Aw, thanks, you guys," Lilee said, blushing.

"Yeah, it's not as terrible as I thought it'd be," Kirstee admitted reluctantly, taking a bite.

"Actually, I'd say it's wonderful," Miss Couri corrected her.

"Yeah, Kirstee, it's wonderful," Kaycee taunted her sister. Then, in a serious tone, she added, "Um, can I have seconds?"

Lilee happily heaped more pasta on Kaycee's plate.

"I'm so glad we got to discover what a talented chef you are!" Yasmin exclaimed.

"So, are you starting to feel better, now that we're starting to fix things?" Fianna asked Lilee.

"I am, but…I still don't know what to do about those articles I destroyed," Lilee sighed.

"Wait, you destroyed their stupid Bratz Magazine articles?" Kirstee demanded. "That's so cool!"

"Kirstee," Miss Couri said warningly.

"I mean, oh, that's too bad."

"Why don't you girls just rewrite your articles?" Miss Couri suggested. "I know it'll be time-consuming, but I'm sure you remember all the cool things you've done here, don't you?"

"Well, sure we do," Jade replied.

"You know, I bet rewriting everything would actually make it better," Yasmin, their resident writer, said. "Sometimes, I'll write a draft and then stick it in my drawer and start from scratch – it's a great way to get a totally fresh take on what you're writing!"

"You know, Lilee, I bet you could do a really funny piece on how you tried to fix things and they kept going wrong," Sasha suggested.

"Actually, I was thinking – if it's okay with all of you – that I might write something on how to make new friends," Lilee replied. "It could be a 'Dos and Don'ts' piece, since I have so many 'Don'ts' to offer!"

"It seems like you've done okay to me," Cloe told her.

"But I owe it all to you girls," Lilee insisted. "I really appreciate how understanding you've been about – well, everything."

"That's what friends are for," Jade replied.

"Okay, I've had enough of this best friends forever nonsense," Kirstee announced. "Kaycee and I are going to our tent. We'll see you in the morning."

With that, she and her twin stomped off.

"What's up with them?" Lilee asked.

"We wonder that every day," Sasha told her. "But some things just can't be explained."

"So, should we get to work on those articles?" Yasmin asked eagerly. She was always excited to get started on a new writing project.

"Actually, you should probably go to bed, for now," Miss Couri interjected. "But what if we went on one last adventure tomorrow?

I think it would make a great addition to your magazine."

"We're always up for adventure," Jade declared.

"So what's the adventure?" Fianna wanted to know.

"White-water rafting!" Miss Couri replied.

"Awesome!" the girls all cheered.

The next morning, they all trekked down to the river again. This time, they all piled into one big, inflatable yellow raft, and Mr Torres steered them through the rapids, twists and turns of the river.

The girls all paddled and also scoped out the sights, getting one last view of the spectacular South American rainforest. They snapped tons of pictures and took notes whenever they stopped at a dry spot for snacks or a brief rest.

"This is definitely the coolest thing we're done on this trip!" Jade squealed as they swerved through the swift-moving current, rocketing down the river with the lush jungle pressing in close on both sides.

"I don't know," Yasmin replied. "We have an awful lot of extremely cool things to choose from."

The next morning, the girls said goodbye to Mr Torres, picked up the Tweevils' excess baggage from base camp and headed back to the airport.

The girls worked on their rainforest-themed pieces for Bratz Magazine for almost the entire plane ride home, and before they even landed, the issue was complete.

By looking back through their digital pictures and pooling their memories of everything that had happened on the trip, the girls had been able to recreate the articles they'd lost – and make them better.

"Now that's teamwork," Cloe said.

"Thanks for helping us write our magazine," Jade said to Lilee. "You did a fantastic job."

"And this is without a doubt the best issue of Bratz Magazine ever," Yasmin added.

"Well, it should be – it's based on the best spring break ever," Sasha declared.

"And you girls are the best friends ever!" Lilee exclaimed.

"Aww!" they all cried.

"And I promise to never, ever, lie to any of you again," Lilee added.

"Your intentions were always good," Yasmin replied. "That's what really matters to us."

"Thanks, you guys," Lilee murmured, tears glinting at the corners of her eyes.

"I'm so glad we got to know you on this trip, Lilee," Cloe said.

"Not as glad as I am that I got to know you," Lilee told her. "I feel so lucky to have friends like you who I know I can always count on – even if I lose our food or set your magazine on fire!"

"Now that is a true measure of friendship," Jade agreed.

The girls burst into giggles, earning them a disapproving look from the flight attendant that only made them laugh harder. It was a long plane ride home, but with best friends like these, the hours flew by!

Read more about the Bratz in
these other awesome books!

Pixie Power
Diamond Road Trip
Pet Project

BRATZ Magazine

the magazine for girls with a PASSION for fashion!

ALL THE LATEST BRATZ & CELEBRITY NEWS!

ALL THE BEST FASHION TIPS & ADVICE!

COOL FEATURES, COMPETITIONS, POSTERS & MORE!

U.K. Customers get 1 issue free!
13 issues for only £29.25
Order online www.titanmagazines.co.uk/bratz
or call 0870 428 8206 (Quoting ref BRZPA1)

U.S. Customers Save 35%!
6 issues for only $19.50
Order online www.titanmagazines.com/bratz
or call 1 877 363 1310 (Quoting ref BRZPA2)